LUCIO SCHINA

THE MYSTERIES OF THE ISLAND OF THARA

ISBN: 978-1-911424-49-9
SKU/ID: 9781911424499

All Rights Reserved. No part of this book can be used or reproduced in any manner whatsoever without written permission from the publisher, except in the case of brief quotations embodied in critical articles or reviews.
A catalogue record for this book is available from the British Library.

Inside illustration: "Sea waves and cliffs" by Vanessa Barbiero
Editor: Wolf Graham
Layout: Wolf Graham
Cover: Wolf Graham
Translation: Charlotte J. March
Publishing Company:
Black Wolf Edition & Publishing Ltd.
Scotland (UK)
www.blackwolfedition.com

Copyright © 2020 by Black Wolf Edition & Publishing Ltd.
and other respective owners identified in this work.
Designs and Patents Act 1988 All rights reserved.
First Edition 2020 - First Printing 2020

I was just finishing packing up the last things to take away when I heard a knock on the door. I had left the smaller objects for last, for fear that they might be lost hidden in who knows what abandoned box in the cellar. A series of objects and curiosities collected in thirty years of research and expeditions around the world. Inside the display case I had arranged them to form a sort of micro museum of anthropological and archaeological sciences. Lithic objects of the Palaeolithic, pestles and remains of Neolithic ceramics, but also amulets, pendants of every kind and shape, figurines representing an incredible pantheon of gods worshipped by the most distant and unknown cultures of the world. A small space in which was enclosed the diversity of our species, beliefs and fears, knowledge and everything that lives beyond perceived reality.

'Is that allowed, Professor?' Ironically my friend and colleague Jørgen Lassen asked, entering without waiting for a reply.

'Come in!' I replied while I was wrapping

every single item to protect it from breakage during transport. 'The ashtray is on the table next to the lamp.'

Jørgen was a hardened smoker and would not enter a closed place without being sure that there was an ashtray and a window inside. I had met him shortly after becoming a researcher; thanks to a scholarship I was invited to spend two years at the Institute of Folk Traditions at the University of Aarhus, Denmark. There was a strong mutual sympathy between us right away. In the faculty of social sciences Jørgen taught social anthropology and chaired the PhD committee, as well as being responsible for the city's archaeological museum. However, the only thing he really loved to do was field research.

'My aim is to broaden as much as possible the knowledge of man and his institutions and, for this, it is necessary to put the backpack on my shoulders and leave...' he confided to me the day we met. 'But traveling...' he added by giving me a vigorous pat on the shoulder, '...allows me above all to try every single brand of cigarette produced in the world.'

Almost three decades had passed since that

day. Of young anthropologists with Marxist ideas remained two distinct professors with white hair and uncertain gait. But the friendship, that one, was as fresh as it was then.

'I'm almost done. I'm going to take this stuff out of here and then give the key back to the caretaker.'

'What are you going to do now?' Jørgen asked me after lighting the cigarette.

I looked at him for a few moments, then I started rolling up the objects in the paper again.

'I don't know. I could travel the world and give interviews, attend conferences, enjoy life traveling. Or maybe I'll buy a little house in the country and start growing salad and tomatoes.'

Jørgen handed me the package and offered me a cigarette.

'Yes!' I answered and reached out to get one. It would have been the second one in my life. The first one, I remember it like it was yesterday, was offered to me the day I graduated.

We remained silent enjoying our last moments together. In the evening I would leave to return to Italy for good.

'Now excuse me, but I still have things to do and I haven't even finished packing at home.'

'See you soon professor,' Jørgen said as he embraced me. There was a touch of emotion in his voice.

Left alone I finished collecting my precious collectibles. I opened all the drawers, pulled out the content and put it in the half empty box. I got in the car and stopped by the caretaker to return the key. I didn't like ceremonies, and if there was the chance to go unnoticed, I didn't ask twice.

By the time I finished packing, the plane was several hours away from departure. I took a shower, made myself a coffee and started opening the yellowed envelopes and reading every little piece of paper that had been lying abandoned in my desk drawers for who knows how long. Notes for lessons, programs to present at meetings, meaningless phrases. There was nothing missing and I smiled to think that the set of those documents could represent the synthesis of what I had been as an anthropologist. Inside some envelopes still sealed and dating back years that I had never opened before, there were invitations to conferences and presentations of exhibitions and museums. Almost all of them asked politely, but firmly, an official answer.

I gathered everything up and put it in a small suitcase where there was still room. In doing so, a little diary fell to the ground. I picked it up and handled it like an object from another planet. The first page had only a date written in pen, July 16, 1976. I was overwhelmed with memories and had to sit down for fear my legs would give way. It all came back to me in a flash. When I returned from that journey, something in me had changed profoundly. I had stopped being certain and had started living on nothing but doubts and questions. I was no longer able to see things as they appeared in the perceivable reality. Because on that journey I had lost the meaning of the term *"reality"* and, with it, the real sense of the world and things. The questions had suddenly multiplied exponentially and what was supposed to be a study trip, perhaps dictated by a romantic component, had turned into a rite of passage.

Back at university I continued to teach the discipline as it had been created and developed by the founding masters, analysing the various currents and always accepting to discuss it with my students without imposing truths that would not be understood. But from that day on, I refused any field research I was offered.

It took me a few minutes to recover from the excitement. I turned two more pages and recognized my handwriting. It was uncertain and hiding a strong anxiety. The diary was interrupted from time to time, giving way to sketches and drawings. Underneath each one there was a little caption. During the three days I spent on the island I had written a diary of about ten pages structured as a fantastic story. I was reminded of the reason for that choice; I wanted to be sure that if it had been read by anyone, it would have been mistaken for something else. I had chosen not to divulge anything about that experience and still today I remain convinced of the goodness of the decision. Not so much because I would be laughed at, but because I felt that those emotions had to be kept inside me and remain a secret forever.

I read it in a few minutes, all in one breath. It was like a light came back on. A story that had marked the entire course of my life. The ending was unbelievable and, although I had written it in my own handwriting, it raised doubts about its authenticity. Too great had been the magic I had experienced, a magic that an age-hardened mind could hardly accept. A story born from curiosity or perhaps from a destiny that had in store for me the most incredible adventure I could imagine. An island hidden among the waves of the northern ocean, a legend handed down for centuries and a secret jealously guarded in the folds of time.

THE MYSTERIES
OF THE ISLAND OF THARA

'Look in the wind at the sinuous lines of her face...'

The first time I heard this story I had just turned ten. The age when imagination and reality come together so naturally that it turns every game into an adventure out of the ordinary. I didn't miss anything to feed my dreamy soul. In the playgrounds I would line up to visit ghost-infested castles and forests inhabited by elves and bizarre spirits. During the summers I spent part of my holidays in my father's hometown, a village by the sea where everything or almost everything seemed to have stopped in the last century. Sometimes, tired of raids with friends, I'd stop at the old dock. While they were busy preparing the boats and nets for their night outings, the fishermen sat me down on a tangle of mooring cables and began to tell me old legends of the sea, where there was no lack a treasure to be salvaged, a huge monster of the depths and old abandoned ships that roamed the stormy seas at night, said to be haunted by the angry spirits of the sailors who had found a violent death there. I would stay and listen with my eyes wide open, losing myself among the images that the mind created and that transformed me into the protagonist of those adventures.

From a young age I had developed a strong interest in reading. On the shelf of my bedroom I had placed, in a well orderly row, a long series of short stories, books belonging to the same literary series, the "Little Mysteries". When in wintertime friends would go out to play ball or hide and seek, I would sink on the couch and fly among disappeared treasures, curses and enchanted places with imagination. The inclination for that literary genre grew over time, gradually transforming itself, maturing and finally resulting in a degree in demo-ethno-anthropological disciplines, with a thesis in popular literature of Northern Europe. Among the many stories I listened to, capable of leaving me open-mouthed, one in particular had struck me to the point of keeping me awake the next four nights. In the darkness of the room, with the blankets pulled up over my nose and the sound of the wind hissing through the branches of the tall trees, sometimes I seemed to hear a faint melody in the distance, a whining whisper similar to the song of remorse of the island of Thara. It was the chance, once I became an adult, that brought that story back to my mind. In the meantime, I had become a researcher at the Faculty of Anthropological Studies at the University of my city. It was the time when I was deepening some studies about the meaning of superstition in modern societies; flipping through an old book of Northern European legends, I happened to read one very similar to the one I had been told many years before. The difference between the versions undoubtedly depended on its oral origins, which over time had made it subject to small and continuous changes. Cleaned of those, however, remained an identical narrative structure. Taken by a teenage curiosity and driven by a professional interest, the following summer I returned to my father's hometown. I wanted to track down the fisherman who first told it to me, to know from whom he had learned that legend and to understand, above all, whether it was considered real or simple fruit of popular imagination.

I came to my old house the following summer; more than twenty years had passed since the last time. I immediately set out on a search. I arrived in the central square and asked the owner of a newsstand. After a moment's hesitation he directed me to the pier. It was a short walk. I did it remembering the alleys and places where I grew up. Not much had changed, the houses and small shops built from old cellars had gone through the years as if nothing had changed, but everything seemed smaller. When I left the village, I continued along a path surrounded by evergreen vegetation, until I saw an immense space open before me that was lost in the blue waters of the ocean. Once I passed a barrier, I headed for the sea and took a look at the boats. It was easy to find his; it was one of the largest and even though the paint had peeled in several places, you could still read the name it was wearing, "Belisama", the ancient and venerated Celtic goddess.

I approached the dock and stopped a short distance away. At that moment, he had turned his back, busy setting up a tangle of nets; very little of the strong and vigorous man remained.

Aged and with his skin made barren by a life spent at sea, the man recognized me after a moment of hesitation. He put on a sweater, got off the boat and invited me to drink in the room that stood inside the pier, a wooden construction similar to the inns found in pirate movies, with the floor and steep wooden furniture, a rudder hanging behind the counter, remains of old fishing nets that came down from the ceiling beams and the rainbow-colored parrot intent on chirping every new customer.

We sat at a table by the window looking out to the sea. The old fisherman put the pipe in his mouth, sucking it in from time to time without lighting it. He ordered a local liqueur and, shortly afterwards, a waitress served us a tray with two small glasses and a bottle without a full three-quarter label. He asked about my father and what I was doing with my life. When I told him, he smiled kindly.

'Then I guess yours isn't just a nostalgia-driven return,' he said as he toasted to the memory of my father.

'In fact,' I replied laconically, raising the glass and swallowing everything in one breath.

He listened with interest to what I told him

about my life and how I had become a rather important anthropologist. When the pleasantries were over, I confided to him the reason for my return.

'The island of Thara...' he repeated in a hoarse voice, sucking his pipe.

I still don't know why I was embarrassed to talk to him about it. I had the feeling that I was asking him to tell me an intimate secret and that we should be careful not to violate a taboo. He remained silent to gather ideas, casting a glance outside that was lost beyond the horizon. Then he began to speak with a firm voice, telling it to me as if only a day had passed since the last time. When he had finished, when asked precisely, he confided to me that he had heard it for the first time from his father, a fisherman like himself, to whom, with typical time sequence, it had been told at an early age by his own. My experience and knowledge of the subject was advising me to reduce it as a mere legend. Although it offered several original cues when compared to others present in Nordic cultures, the structure retained all its characteristics. It was likely that my mind, inclined to reject life as a set of events subject only to rational laws, wanted to keep alive a simple suggestion. I closed the notebook I hadn't written any notes on. Challenged, I proposed a final toast before saying goodbye; it was extraordinary to realize only at that moment that I ignored the name of one of the people who had most influenced my life choices. I looked at my watch; it was almost time for the ferry to depart and I didn't want to risk being late for boarding. I asked for the bill and went to get my wallet; it was then that the old fisherman put his hand on my arm, making me realize with his eyes that he really kept a secret inside himself that was about the history of the island of Thara. Before talking he offered me another couple of drinks, he lit his pipe, which he was proud of because it was carved by himself with a rare local wood. A little whitish cloud soon formed around us.

'I was eight years old when my father told me the legendary story of the island of Thara. As we were having breakfast, he told me with a pinch of pride that I was ready to listen to it. He was wrong! Contrary to what he thought, I was deeply disturbed. I ran to hide under the covers for fear and stayed there all morning. Driven by curiosity, however, the next day I asked him if that story was true; he simply spread his arms out, pointing to me a yellowed picture of my grandfather. He added with a smile that he had been caught by my own curiosity at the time. With him, however, my grandfather was much more talkative. He told him about a strange encounter during a night fishing trip. Together with a new crew member, he was given the task of controlling the nets while they were being thrown into the water, to prevent them from getting caught. Waiting to pull the catch on board, they started talking to kill time. Between a chat and a cigarette, the guy told him the story in great detail. And that's where the word-of-mouth chain breaks. In an enigmatic tone, in fact, the man added that it was not a legend, but an experience really lived in first person.'

I was silent just like I used to be when I was a teenager. This time, though, I was in doubt whether or not to believe him. After all, the element of novelty represented by the mysterious character who lives the story in first person, could be itself functional to the story, an element often used to artificially increase its credibility. I was absorbed in my thoughts when the old man apologized and got up from his chair. His crew were waiting for him outside, ready to set sail on a fishing trip.

'The sea is calm and the winds are favourable!' He greeted me warmly, resting his hand on my shoulder, while with the other he held his smoking pipe firmly. He put on his shoulder a huge backpack and made to leave the room, receiving the greetings and good luck of those present. Before the door closed behind him, he turned one last time and said enigmatically, 'And every wind holds a story.'

Words that were confused with the parrot's chirp.

The ferry to the mainland would leave in half an hour. It was the only daily journey it made, so there were only a few minutes left to reflect.

But think about what?

I took stock of the situation. The next day I was to give an important seminar to which I had been invited for months. The university had provided accommodation and had left a small vademecum in the hotel with timetables and travel around the city. I stared at the liquor glass, half full. The bottle was grape red in colour; it gave off a slightly sweetish odour and retained a rum flavour that had been aged for years. With my fingertips I made it twirl, bending it until it almost poured the alcohol on the table. I thought for another minute and then, reclining my head backwards, I sent it down with a firm sip, grabbed my backpack and headed towards the main harbour, where the crossing boats were moored. I approached one of the larger ones; it was a boat about twenty yards long, with a small cockpit, a deck, and benches scraped from the water to port and starboard. Stains of discoloured paint came out here and there along the sideboards, a sign that originally the boat must have been a very pronounced dark blue. A guy in his 50s showed up. The appearance was far from respecting the clichés of the brave captain. No cap with a sailor's visor, no long white beard and no surly character. He dressed in a large yellow sweater and a pair of wool trousers, and had a large mass of messy curly hair on his head. He gave me permission to come aboard and greet me with a friendly smile.

'If you want to visit the islands off the promontory you've found the right person. We can set sail in half an hour. In this season, then, they offer beautiful natural spectacles.'

I asked him if he could make his way to the island of Thara; the expression on his face became questioning, but he went back to relax a moment after hearing what I was offering him for the crossing.

'We leave in 20 minutes, time to set course and refuel.'

'Perfect!' I simply responded, giving a slight nod of approval with my hand.

While the powerful motor propellers drew a white trail into the sea and the ferry headed north towards the mainland, our boat turned east, with a slight wind in the stern, towards the small and almost forgotten island of Thara. After passing the small islands nearby, the sea became frizzier and the captain shouted to push the engines at full power. All I did during the crossing was watch the sea. I shut myself off altogether. I had planned a study trip but now, lost among the waves and an endless horizon, I realized I had given up the role of researcher the moment I stepped on board. The reason that prompted me to visit the island of Thara was unknown to me, yet it seemed natural to me as if the mind had programmed it many years earlier, only to make it dormant in the years to come. I was taking a leap in the dark and I knew I had to. I had not carried out any kind of preliminary study, neither geographical nor historical anthropological. All I had with me was the little book that contained the story, a small drawing kit and a diary for personal notes. Whether in those few faded pages there was a fictionalized account of an event that had actually happened, or a fictionalized story that over time had turned into legend, I would have discovered it once I landed and set foot on the island. I remember, as if it were now, that the view of the pristine sea of the north had cleared my mind of all thoughts, making me tune in to the natural elements that surrounded me; it was as if an inner call was guiding me, a feeling that I felt clearly during the journey. I could hear something akin to a hiss, a slight melody mixing in the wind. Its origins were obscure to me and I didn't understand if it came from outside or, on the contrary, if it came from inside. It was imposing, embracing, and it traced the path I was walking down. As evening fell and the sun's reflections on the waves turned into a bright rosy hue, I saw the island's outlines blurred from the horizon. A crewman warned me we'd be arriving at our destination within minutes. I used that little time to re-read the legend one last time. It was called "The Echo of Remorse". The plot weaves with wise ambiguity reality and supernatural; I deliberately use these terms in a conventional way, not having the certainty of where the barrier that divides it from its opposite rests.

Paragraph 1

Those who are accustomed to sailing the stormy seas of the Atlantic are aware of the existence of a small island located in the far north of the continent called Europe, far from the coast and modernity. It's famous for being a place with a double soul. During the day surrounded by a clear blue sky, with fresh breezes blowing from the sea, fishy and untouched like few others. At night a cold place, beaten by a wind that brings with it sinister howls. At sunset the sea turns black, taking on the restless appearance of a crazy dancing satyr. On the west side, surrounded by greenery, there was a fishing village; from there, crossing an impassable path, you could reach a natural bay, a perfect place to protect boats during storms. The village was surrounded by lush countryside as far as the eye could see. On the opposite side stood an isolated villa, built half a century earlier. The falling facade gave it a ghostly air. It was built on the models of the old colonial villas of neo-classical style. The window panes had come down; a few isolated fragments resist-

ed the time, lying on the original frame, which had become soaked with moisture. The plaster had almost completely peeled off the main facade, facing the sea, and had left the concrete curtain bare, which had deep cracks. The inner garden, a splendid aesthetic ornament one day, was covered with brushwood due to neglect.

The boat moored in a natural inlet. Before going down I made the last arrangements with the commander, who showed me the way to the old village. He'd be back to pick me up in three days. In the meantime, the sky had turned grey and the warm rays of the sun had been replaced by a damp cold that I had begun to feel just before landing. I put my backpack on my shoulder, put on my scarf and hat and walked down the path. I crossed a dense woodland, a wild and unspoilt landscape, alternating with expanses of lawns and areas rich in moss as the hills descended towards the stacks that plunged steeply into the ocean. After about an hour, I finally reached the village, composed of small stone houses neatly arranged along a central street; they all had sloping roofs covered with grass and soil, with the chimney on one side. I got over it quickly and came to the main square. I didn't meet a soul on the way. Even though the locals must not have been used to receiving foreigners, it didn't surprise me much, because the commander had told me that in summer, a couple of times a month, he used to transport someone to the island, mostly lovers of unspoilt places far from the normal tourist routes. In the meantime, evening had fallen and the cold had become more intense. I entered the only inn present. There was no time to visit the places that at first glance seemed to me pervaded by an aura of magic, so different from the everyday life I was used to. I rang the bell on the counter and immediately a girl came out of a back room, asking me something in a local dialect I'd never heard before. I attempted in vain with English first and then Danish, I finally tried to make myself understood with gestures. Finally, the girl understood, smiled at me, took a key from the cabinet and waved to me to follow her; she led me upstairs, stopping in front of a room door. Then she sat me down and kept smiling and made some gestures that I translated into 'If you're hungry, come down and ask for me.' I smiled at her as a sign that I understood. After all, I was enjoying the situation I was in. Even the local dialect contributed to making that place so far from the world I was used to.

I put the clothes in the drawers, took a shower and went downstairs for dinner. The food was served to me in wooden bowls. The menu was based on fish with various side dishes of vegetables. The wine cup was also made of inlaid wood. Beautiful royal coats of arms stood out on the walls of the room, lit by a huge fireplace on which a heap of burning embers burned. I tried in vain to make the girl understand the term "coffee", but I was unsuccessful and resigned myself to the fact that I would not drink any until I returned. Tired of the day, I went up to my room, prepared myself for the night and began writing a diary, organizing it as if it were the plot of a novel. I wrote the first pages with a wealth of details, pervaded by the feeling of having fallen back in time, in a remote place protected by the immense North Sea. Before falling asleep I turned off the light and closed the window shutters; it was in the silence that I slowly felt myself captured. Among the howls of the wind I had the sensation of hearing a voice coming from outside, I woke up sitting at the base of the bed; I thought it strange that at that hour there might be someone in the garden. I looked down, but in the semi-darkness I saw no one; I took one last quick look, closed the shutters again and went back to bed, convinced that I had mistaken the noise of the wind for something different. I closed my eyes and fell fast asleep.

I woke up in the morning with a warm sun peeping through the white clouds. While I was having breakfast, I mentally organized the day. I would initially visit the inhabited part of the island, until I reached the mill which was on the bank of a stream, whose large shovels I could see in the distance. In the afternoon I would move along the nature trails that started on the west side of the village and branched off into the interior. I would visit the eastern area and the abandoned villa the next day, stopping along the main stacks to draw the landscape. After eating, I went back to my room to get my backpack; I put on my sunglasses to check that the lenses were clean, approached the window and opened it to change the air. Looking out, a fleeting image passed in front of my eyes.

Convinced of how my mind had not given importance to an apparently insignificant event, I was intrigued to realize that something had deeply disturbed me. I thought back to the night before and the noise that had woken me up; I had tried to make it look like a joke in my mind, but I knew it was a convenient explanation. Something else had been confused with the wind, or perhaps, I imagined, travelled with it; I could not properly call it a voice, but a graceful whisper of feminine origin. It seemed inconceivable but, it was as if it had deliberately waited for the wind to start its singing, a romantic explanation that almost made me smile. Going back to visit the places of my childhood had awakened in me the dreamy child I had been. In the end I was convinced that I was mistaken; on the other hand, fatigue may have played a bad trick on me, forcing me to look for an explanation for a phenomenon originated by a simple auditory suggestion. However, I continued to perceive a feeling similar to anxiety, which warned me of something that permeated the reality of the island and had nothing to do with rationality. I went down to the dining room and asked the maid some questions, I was curious to know if there were other guests in the inn, especially a girl; without saying anything, she lowered her gaze before making me realize that at the moment I was the only customer and that the other rooms were empty. I gave thanks and came out quickly.

I spent the morning following the pre-established itinerary: I visited the village, the main square where the weekly market was held and the place where the fish was processed and preserved. Around me there was an apparent calm, the few inhabitants were busy with some business and no one seemed to notice my presence. I stopped in a small grocery store, finally found a man who understood my language and asked him directions on the paths that opened at the end of the village. He showed me the direction to follow, explaining that it was a long path that cut the island in two and ended not far from the villa. I pushed myself over a shaky old fence and started walking. I reached the edge of the hill, where I visited a church dating back to the first half of the 19th century; it was a modest stone building, with a still working bell tower facing east; at the back, bordered by a low fence, there was a well-kept garden and, beyond the small cemetery, with gravestones planted in the ground; the oldest ones, which were in the middle, were slightly bent, with inscriptions made illegible by the passage of time. Before going on I said goodbye to the shepherd, who was busy working in the small vegetable garden at the time. He was very old, curved on his shoulders and his eyes were sunken from age. I descended the opposite side of the island; after about two hours I reached the high cliffs that plunged into the sea. The foam of the waves breaking on the coast was a too wild and spectacular image for me not to be fascinated by it. I pulled out a sheet of smooth paper and a pencil, mounted the small tripod and placed the support frame on it. I was familiar with freehand drawing and used to take everything I needed with me on study trips. My field journals ended up being a mixture of notes and sketches in chiaroscuro. I stared for a long time at the image I had in front of me; I let myself go waiting to catch the vibrations that hovered in the air and then, suddenly, I began to draw with decisive strokes the motionless natural elements and blurred those in motion. I was so bewitched by what I observed that I almost fell into a kind of trance; but as the night before, I was awakened again by the wind. I was surprised to see how the weather conditions on the island changed so suddenly, every time the sun was covered by clouds. During the crossing the boat's captain had told me about a strong wind that used to get up every night on the island. To create an aura of mystery, he added that a local belief traced its origin back to the sighs of a sea goddess, who was enchanted by the beauty of those wonderful places. From this belief, he concluded, the island was nicknamed "Island of Sighs".

Paragraph 2

The island was constantly beaten by a strong mistral wind, which rose at dusk and continued until sunrise. Suddenly it was quiet and the days became favourable for the fishermen and the few shepherds who led their flocks on the wide green expanses to the north. But every night, without a single break in two days, the wind would blow again, restless and wild. Soon rumours began to circulate that the island was infested with evil spirits and that the wind was the torment for a guilt that the inhabitants were guilty of. A pastor was called from the mainland and soon settled on the island. A small church was built on the east side and the inhabitants began to attend it with the hope that prayers could quiet the spirits and bring serenity back into the community.

At dusk I decided to interrupt the drawing; I put it back in order and put the backpack on again. To return to the inn I chose a path that ran along the cliff, from which it was possible to admire the swirl of the waves of the sea and listen to the song of the seagulls as they danced suspended between the currents of the north. Halfway through I found myself passing in front of the villa, I had planned to visit it the next day, believing it to be far from the beaten path. I deviated from the route and passed the main gate; the boundary walls had given way in several places and a lane with remains of flowerbeds on the sides led to the entrance. I checked that there was someone inside; I saw that a rocking chair was attached to a tree and kept clean, but except for that little clue, there didn't seem to be a living soul. I took a couple more looks and just took a few more pictures before I went back to the main trail. Slowly I was mentally reconstructing the map of the places described in the legend. I was surprised to discover how much it had to do with reality; even the emotional aspect that the island conveyed was similar to that which inspired the reading of the story. It was possible that the suggestion made me feel sensations originated unconsciously based on my knowledge, but I was beginning to believe in the possibility that the island of Thara was really hiding a secret and that this had been entrusted to a legend so as not to bury it under the sand of time.

After passing the church again I made my way to the village and it was at that moment that an icy shiver ran down my back from the neck down, like a sudden electric shock. I planted my feet on the ground and stood still listening; behind me I had heard the same hiss as the night before. I turned with a snap; the wind had meanwhile started to blow hard again. My hair was fluttering madly tickling my cheeks and ending up in front of my eyes. Like the night before I didn't see anyone, but this time I was sure I felt something, at least as real as the terror I'll be in an ice grip. Confused among the noises generated by the wind was a woman's voice, the exact same voice. Soft and low-toned, it approached and brushed me as if it were transported, while its origin was lost in the unknown. I closed my eyes and listened, trying to isolate her. I sensed it in the background and would say it was a song; the sound of the words was unknown to me and I was unaware of their meaning. I locked myself in the heavy vest and, slowly, I was able to get back on the road. The voice accompanied me to the threshold of the inn. I was restless for the rest of the evening. Immediately after dinner I continued writing in my diary. The silence was abruptly interrupted by the shutter of a window, which started banging violently on the wall after losing its support. I opened to fasten it to the hook and again, out of the darkness, I heard that sound. I closed my eyes, looking for maximum concentration. It sounded like a song, like a sinister music with tight lips or something similar to the call of a mermaid, a mythological and terrifying character, who in ancient times was able to sink ships with the sensual gaze of a virgin, whose angel's smile hid teeth as sharp as blades and from whose lips came out the hypnotic notes of the song of death.

I spent a restless night in nightmares. From the darkness I could see a sinuous shape approaching, which slowly took on the features of a woman; she was dressed in white, the colour of her skin pale. She called me, extending her arms sensually and signalling to come closer. The smile hid a malignant expression; the eyes were as black as a starless night, while the hair waved like restless snakes. I woke up suddenly, exhaling violently, as if I had held my breath and was about to suffocate to death. I wiped my sweaty brow, got up and freshened up. Morning had come up outside and dim light was filtering through the window shutters. The day was gloomy and the pouring rain was accompanied by lightning and sinister thunder, high grey clouds overlooked the sky, immobile, shapeless clusters similar to jagged mountain ranges. This time the wind had anticipated its arrival, crossing the invisible barrier between day and night. It crept between the interstices of the doors, wedging himself between the tiny openings of the old wooden frames; he whistled and panting like a wounded animal. I went down to the dining room, where I tried to talk to the waitress again. She was frightened to see my restless expression, but even this time she didn't seem to understand what I was asking her. At the moment of serving me she took care to keep her eyes on the ground, but in the end, while she was clearing the table and certain that no one was watching her, she grabbed something out of her pocket and handed it to me with a stealthy gesture. I got up like it was nothing and went out of the inn heading out the back, where I sat on a wooden bench sheltered under a large bush. Only then I decided to open the crumpled note; in the local language there was a word written, nothing else. Disappointed and bewildered, I went back to my room, grabbed my backpack and headed to the village store. The streets were deserted because of the incessant rain coming down from the leaden sky. Sitting behind the counter, I saw a man who was very far ahead of his age flipping through a newspaper, I greeted him with a wave of my hand trying to catch his attention, showed him the piece of paper and asked him politely if he could translate its contents. Without opening his mouth, he looked in his pocket for a pair of long-sighted glasses and, once found, placed them on his nose with very slow movements. He took the note between two wrinkled fingers, squeezing his eyes slightly to focus. He thought about it for a moment then, lifting his gaze as he took off his glasses, he stared at me.

'Priest,' he said in a hoarse voice and a strong Nordic accent as he returned the ticket with a trembling hand.

'The pastor...' I echoed him by running my hand through my hair. I gave thank and put the card back in my pocket before I left. As if it was nothing, the old man went back to leafing through the paper.

At the top of the hill the rain came down more vehemently, lashed by a wind blowing more violently. The trees swung like the waves of a stormy ocean, while the colours of nature had lost their shine and taken on gloomy hues. The shaky door to the little barn was shaking like it was about to fly off. I went into the church. There was a strange quiet atmosphere; the outside noises had subsided. I took a few steps, passed the tiny central vault and looked to the right. I went past the shrine and stopped; on the right I saw a man with his head bowed and his hands folded in prayer. As soon as he sensed my presence, he turned around distractedly looking at me, then he came back to cross his hands holding an object. The silence that enveloped the interior made the environment suspended in time. I felt distant from everything and felt an almost tactile discomfort; it was like being at the mercy of an uncontrollable nature that had unleashed its wrath. The light filtering through the frosted windows created shadows in the corners and small spaces between the naves. On the walls were still visible the remains of ancient frescoes depicting the expulsion of man from Eden, which came back to life when soft reflections of the sun, making a breach in the clouds, penetrated through the side windows. I had a sudden feeling of cold; to look for some warmth I squeezed myself into my jacket, hiding my face inside my raised lapel. I decided to sit and wait. After a few minutes the man got up and approached me, beckoning me to follow him as far as behind the altar, where a side entrance opened. The footsteps echoed like the chimes of a clock set in the tower of a castle. In the shrine a door led into a tiny room; inside there was a bed with a bedside table next to it. The furniture was limited to a small table and two chairs. I sat after him. I heard a wheeze and only a few whispered words. I didn't understand their meaning. The pastor lit a candle, put it in the middle of the table to make light and began to speak,

'I saw you go past the church and walk up to the cliff. I know you're a foreigner who's just arrived on the island. There are very few of them coming around here now. But I knew you'd come and talk to me. I've been waiting for you.'

There was a brief silence.

'His name was made to me in the village...'

'About what?'

'I wish I knew...' I said in an uncertain tone of voice.

'Something's bothering you,' resumed, 'because you're looking for answers to questions you don't understand or maybe don't ask yourself properly.'

I tried to gather my thoughts.

'That voice I hear father...'

The man had a gasp. He took a deep breath and closed his eyes; after regaining control, he said in a deep tone, 'A voice, or perhaps a way not to forget.'

I didn't understand the meaning of the sentence, but I had the proof I was looking for. The strange phenomena I felt were not the result of imagination. What I thought was a legend had suddenly turned into a real story.

'Don't forget?' I just asked. I didn't want to force his answers, I just wanted to humour him.

'We all have the duty to remember, those who live on this island know it well. The atonement of sin passes through remembrance,' he sighed again, 'and remorse.'

I had no time to add anything else. The pastor got up, left the room and returned to his contemplation. His words had had the effect of a hangover; I was confused and at the mercy of events, but something inside me told me that I was on the right track.

I went back to the village. I locked myself in my room and tried to put order in my head. Something had to have happened and that something must have triggered consequences that would change the course of existence on the island forever. Now I understood that the wind was not only a natural phenomenon and that a higher will had to lie behind it, able to control the elements of nature and bend them to its own will. The myths of all pre-Christian religions sketched animistic divinities and the Nordic one was far too rich in them. But imagining that myth could transmigrate into everyday reality would have forced me to rethink every structure of collective human thought, replacing it with a system capable of going beyond any classifying will, in which the need for a dichotomous model became useless and in which the only divine design was one as a synthesis of the whole. A system in which the barriers of time and space lost all physical and mental consistency, becoming abstract concepts. To accept to question centuries of knowledge and knowledge, however, I needed to unravel the mystery and understand what was hidden behind the wind-blown song. In the pastor's words there had to be the key to unlocking the mystery. They were enigmatic but full of meaning. I was missing one last piece to discover the truth and I was sure I would find it in the villa, along with the answers I was looking for.

Paragraph 3

The pastor, a man of faith and profound humanistic culture, began researching the history of the island. He found evidence of a community of fishermen who, from the mainland, had decided to set up a community offshore, in a place where they could live in peace from their only work. The waters were very rich in fish and the interior of the island allowed a modest cultivation of some fruit and vegetable plants. Everyone was called to donate part of their belongings and share them with others. It seemed a happy community, until an inexplicable event put an end to peace and harmony.

The boat that was going to take me off the island was only a few hours away. There was no way I could have postponed my departure. But the desire to know was too strong, I felt the need, especially now that I felt so close to the truth. I wanted to know from whom, or what, the voice that travelled on the wings of the wind originated. I decided to go out, relying solely on instinct and a dormant sixth sense that, since I arrived, I felt awakened. I walked for about an hour; something had pushed me to the opposite end of the island, near the high cliffs. The sky was clear again, but the wind, which until then had only tormented the inhabitants at night, had never stopped blowing, saturating the air with a deep anxiety. The visual perception changed, as if a reddish fog had descended from above; the moans had become more acute, as if sudden lashes were able to penetrate your mind. It was not a chant, nor a hiss, what I now distinctly felt was a litany of suffering.

The villa was a structure once inhabited by a rich lord; a huge two-storey farmhouse and a garden bordered by elegant fountains at the four corners, adorned with marble statues depicting classical gods, now half hidden by climbing vegetation; of the fences remained only the signs of the walls now collapsed, which drew a rectangular floor plan just mentioned in the ground that from the size must have had a more decorative function than defensive; this made understand the non-confrontational relations of the owner towards the inhabitants of the village.

I walked through the ruins and went inside;

I went around the house looking at the most hidden corners but I found nothing strange; I didn't know exactly what I was looking for. The villa was in a state of total abandonment; I carefully inspected the avenues, uprooted the plants and brought to light the fountains, but I found no clue that could be useful to me. The sound of the footsteps was covered by the wind and the sound of the voice that repeated its moaning relentlessly. Like an obsession I felt an unknown anxiety grow. I tried to plug my ears with the palms of my hands, but that whisper seemed to find no obstacle before it, as if it were able to cross every barrier until it blinded my consciousness like a fog on a moor. Suddenly, I isolated a noise coming from the other side of the villa. I quickly walked the west perimeter until I found myself near the entrance. I saw a man sitting on the old deckchair under the big tree. He dressed in dark pants and wore a horizontal striped sweater. Deep wrinkles marked his face from his eyes to his forehead; gusts of wind had disrupted his few white hairs.

Paragraph 4

A rich landowner lived on the island. The son behaved as if he was the master of everything, mocking the efforts and sacrifices that the inhabitants made to try to survive. It happened one cold winter evening in the inn. The boy entered accompanied by two friends who had just arrived from the mainland. All three of them were drunk and hiding hunting knives in the inside pockets of their jackets. They started bothering the master's daughter, until big words came out and a fight almost broke out. Luckily, the intervention of some clients restored calm. The three boys gave up their intentions and retired to the estate to sober up.

'You!' I exclaimed surprised.

'Sit and observe,' he replied with the same deep intonation he had used in church.

'Why are you here?' I asked stunned.

'I come here every day. I listen, I pray and ask forgiveness.'

'Forgiveness"? Forgiveness for what?'

The pastor didn't turn around. He was staring at something in front of him and seemed captured by it.

'It happened many years ago; I don't even remember the exact date anymore. At the time this place was almost uninhabited. Only very few exiles had decided to put down roots and start a new life. Most of them were simple fishermen and small craftsmen. But among them was a young and arrogant boy, son of a rich and well-known landowner, who had bought a large plot of land on the west side of the island. He behaved as if he was the owner of everything, mocking the efforts and sacrifices that the inhabitants made to try to survive. It happened one cold winter evening in the inn. The boy entered accompanied by two friends who had just arrived from the mainland; they were all three drunk and hid hunting knives in the inside pocket of their jackets. They began to pester the master's daughter heavily, until big words flew out and there was almost a fight. Luckily, the intervention of some clients restored calm. It seemed the three of them had given up their intentions and retired to the estate to sober up.'

His face was pulled, as if telling the story caused him pain; he let go, resting his neck on the deckchair, I was surprised to hear him and he used the same words I had read, simply repeating them. But how was it possible to imagine such a thing, when the origins of history had to go back at least three centuries?

He resumed his story, in a relaxed tone.

'But it wasn't like that. They waited for the inn to be empty and everyone to retire to their homes. The girl came out last; her father had already gone home when she was kidnapped and taken away, this far, where we are now sitting and talking. The boy, the most violent of the three, pulled out his knife and began to threaten her; I let you imagine the terror that struck her, she was frightened to death and trembled like a leaf. When the alarm was raised in the village, no one knew where he was. She backed back, went through the gate and headed back to the edge of the ground. The boy, blinded by alcohol, kept threatening her fiercely trying to get close to her, wielding that damn shiny blade. The escape routes were blocked. The only thing she had to do to save herself was to give herself to those three animals and lose her honour, when the last step back was fatal; the earth collapsed under her feet, she lost her balance and fell down the cliff. The boy, once he realized what had happened, threw the knife on the ground, knelt on the edge and stared with his waxy face at the black abyss that had just swallowed that innocent soul. He understood then the gravity of his gesture and, in that instant, he was struck by an electrocution. Everyone in the village knew, but no one dared go against him and testify at the trial. The investigation was dismissed as "suicide" and the girl's body was never recovered. And it was then, at the very moment the judge read the verdict, that the entire community was condemned by a court placed above the earthly will. From that day on, the wind began to blow every night, becoming a constant element in the life of the island. You could hear it suddenly get up and start howling like a hungry beast in search of food. It wasn't long afterwards that some fishermen began to hear the reflection of a voice, a sound similar to a lament, which came with the wind and disappeared with it. That's why the island was soon christened "the island of sighs".

'Does that mean...'

'Yes,' replied the pastor as he continued staring into the sea without giving me a chance to finish the question, 'that sigh you hear is her lament, the same sigh that she emitted a moment before she fell off that damn cliff. It comes back to remember our faults and condemn us for her death. No one has left this place since. Our verdict is read every day, every moment, by a supreme judge who governs our lives. The condemnation is to continue to remember the tremendous guilt we have been guilty of, which has made us cowardly people.'

'Her last sigh,' I said quietly to myself, 'but how do you know all these things?'

The pastor turned around, his eyes were shiny and lost in the pain he was carrying inside; he hinted at a desperate smile.

'Because I'm responsible for that girl's death. I distinctly heard his excruciating wailing a moment before she lost her balance and vanished into thin air. I will never forget her look full of anguish, I don't know why she gave it, but I know that from that moment on it turned into a litany of death, a litany that screams in my mind without a moment of peace, accompanying me everywhere, day and night, all the way to my nightmares, endlessly repeating themselves always the same. Since then I feel the echo of remorse pulsating inside me and I try to carry the full weight of the tragedy through prayer and meditation. On this island our God seems not to listen to our pleas and I believe He has abandoned us to this sad fate. This one I hold in my hands – he showed me what I had also seen in church, a hair tie – I picked it up where she fell. After that night, torn by guilt, I decided to embrace religion and, after a few years, I began my work as a pastor. Now I pray every moment for forgiveness for me and on behalf of the whole community of this place. I do so in the hope that one day her spirit will finally find peace. If it ever happens and if we are ever granted forgiveness, I will understand it from the wind, which will soothe its anger with the same mysterious diligence with which it began to torment our souls. For this reason,' he concluded crying, 'during the day I come back to sit here, just as I did that night many years ago, and in the evening, I lock myself in the sacristy and welcome those who come in search of comfort.'

After caressing me and carving the sign of the cross on my forehead with his finger, the pastor waved me away. I walked towards the village, I felt a deep anxiety; every word weighed like a boulder, the horror seen in the girl's eyes had taken hold of him, branding him for eternity. When selfishness and human stupidity had condemned an innocent soul, a higher conscience had decided to wash away the infamy by throwing the guilty ones a terrible punishment, the most terrible: to make their foolishness manifest.

I'd unveiled the mystery I'd carried inside since childhood. The story of a murder that was not supposed to have guilty and that time had turned into legend, to be handed down from father to son and used as a pedagogical form, to introduce into the new generations the moral precepts that give meaning to the social group to which they belong. A reality with the mark of ignominy, which had been allowed to slip from consciousness and hide in the timeless folds of a legend. The wind had done nothing but carry that sigh, a breath that did not hide joy, but terror and madness, having slowly infected the inhabitants of the island. In the melancholy silence of that afternoon, I transcribed the account in my travel diary. The certainties

I had fed on had suddenly crumbled. Unveiling the secret of the island of Thara had opened up in me a universe of knowledge in which rational and emotional thought merged to create a new synthesis. The reality I was observing was nothing more than a tissue paper cover that hid a mysterious essence that went beyond time and space, subject to rules that were beyond my comprehension. The sense of anguish that had taken hold of me had torn apart many of my certainties, but had revealed the only truth I had ever sought.

When I got off to return the key, I crossed the maid for the last time; she did not look back at me. In the dining room the old owner sat on the sofa in front of the kitchen. In the irrational logic of events, I call it irrational only by convention, he could only be the father of the murdered girl. And if so, the maid with whom I had tried so many times to establish a conversation, could only be the victim that someone had wanted to sacrifice at the altar of their arrogance.

Before taking the path to the pier, I turned around one last time and watched in silence. There seemed to be an apparent calm reigning in the village. The streets were deserted and from the rooftops I could see the smoke coming out of the chimneys. After about an hour's walk I arrived at my destination. The boat moored a few minutes late. Nobody got off. I quickly boarded the boat and we sailed with a slightly rippling sea. The captain greeted me with a wave of his hand while a sailor was tinkering with ropes near the mast. I went down to the deck and sat down in the inner room. I looked out through the porthole made opaque by the saltiness. As the island became smaller and smaller in my eyes, I could still distinguish the unspoilt green of the hill, while the wind, which had become so strong in my mind that I could almost touch it with my hand, did not hint at subsiding.

'I hope you had a pleasant stay,' the sailor reproached me without ceasing to tinker with the ropes.

'Apart from the unsteady weather,' I answered without emphasis with a smile of circumstance, 'I spent three very restful days.'

The sailor turned to the other side and began to babble to himself.

His words, however, came to me clearly.

'What some fools find in staying alone on a desert island, I say...'

It was like plunging into an abyss that suddenly opened underfoot. I heard the light thud of the diary and the pen falling on the floor. Hands motionless and stiff, the frost creeping up on my back and coming up over my shoulders. Still in shock, I ran outside and leaned against the stern rail. I looked in the direction of the village, trying to catch a glimpse of the roofs of the houses in the distance; but no matter how much I leaned out, I saw nothing but the top of the hill. As the boat was slowly manoeuvring over the bay and into the open sea, I had the impression that I could see the remains of a building.

'What is that ruin?' I pretended to see it for the first time.

The sailor put the palm of his hand on his forehead to protect his eyes and leaned forward in the direction I had indicated.

'There used to be a church on the island,' he replied, 'but the pastor, its last inhabitant, died about three centuries ago. It has since been declared completely uninhabited. What you see are the ruins that remain.'

Paragraph 5

The next morning the inn owner's daughter was reported missing. There was research and legal experts were brought in from the mainland. After two days, however, the girl was reported missing. Some traces brought her back to the top of the hill, near the great cliff that jumps into the ocean. No one could ever explain the dynamic and in the end, the case was dismissed as suicide. There were rumours that the girl was in love with a boy, but he had not returned her love. The pastor concluded that the whispering that was heard during the nights was the song of the girl, now happy in the place where she lived. From that day on, the island became known as the "island of sighs".

I set foot on dry land several hours later. I remained silent for the rest of the crossing, refusing to look for a rational explanation which, today as then, my conscience would have rejected.

After saying goodbye to the captain and the crew, I headed towards the quay where the ferry was moored, which was shuttling back and forth with the mainland. I bought a ticket, took a seat in the small bar and waited for the moorings to be removed. When I left the mainland I had a feeling of awakening, the same feeling I feel now more than twenty years later. It was as if my body was awakening from a long sleep; my breath was returning to normal, the sounds around it crisp and ringing. What I had experienced only in the morning appeared to me as an echo of blurred memories, which suddenly emerged from a sedimented and almost forgotten time. Who or what had allowed me to live an experience so out of time and logic would remain forever an impenetrable mystery. The island of Thara had forced me to redraw the perceptual limits of the universe, widening them out of all proportion and collapsing all conviction like so many twigs swept away by a storm wind. Everything, from that moment on, had begun to appear different to me, immensely smaller; space had turned into a meaningless word, as had the idea of the linear flow of time. My body and my spirit had managed to hover in the air, overcoming the limits that we think are the last outposts of perceptible experience to reach another dimension, where the synthesis of the primordial order is located and where the ancestral vibrations of all existing emotions are born. I made myself a receptacle and allowed a foreign force to grab my soul and lead it to the origin of an event that had marked the course of my existence, leaving me the decision whether or not to unravel the mystery that, until then, had lived dormant. An experience that made me free to observe reality as it really appears if one has the desire to discover what lies behind the veil that we build ourselves day after day, like putting up a wall that becomes our mental prison for the rest of our lives.

Now there is silence; everything around it dissolves and loses consistency.

I remain suspended in the void for a few moments; when I return to hear the relaxed sound of my breath the images take on their original forms. I close the diary and I have the feeling that a passage out of time is dissolving like a fog at the sight of the first sun. A honking sound shakes the numbness out of me; my taxi just entered the driveway. From the window I signal that I am ready; during the journey to the airport the driver talks to me about everything and nothing but my mind is elsewhere and I don't listen to a word. I watch the world from the open window and let the cool late summer wind caress my face. After not even an hour, I'm at my destination. As I climb the stairs of the plane, I turn one last time to look back at my past, a whole phase of life coming to an end; staring at the rosy horizon a last memory resurfaces as if I were back on the boat. It goes back to the moment before the contours of the island disappeared completely, swallowed up by the horizon; I wanted to take a picture but had to give up because of the strong jolts caused by the rough sea. After a few minutes, when the last strip of land had vanished along with its mysteries, the wind had suddenly died down, giving way to a warm breeze. Before the currents changed direction, however, I had the impression of hearing a woman's light whisper, a sweet melody carried by the wind, confused among the songs of the sea spirits.

INDEX

✎ INDEX ✎

Prologue	*3*
The mysteries of the island of Thara	*11*
Paragraph 1	*25*
Paragraph 2	*35*
Paragraph 3	*47*
Paragraph 4	*51*
Paragraph 5	*61*